ISBN 1 85854 285 5
© Brimax Books Ltd 1996. All rights reserved.
Published by Brimax Books Ltd, Newmarket, England CB8 7AU 1996.
Printed in Dubai.

# HEIDI

## JOHANNA SPYRI

ADAPTED BY

# JOHN ESCOTT

ILLUSTRATED BY

# ANDREW TUDOR

Brimax · Newmarket · England

# Heidi

Johanna Spyri was born in a little village near Zurich, Switzerland in 1829. She wrote many books for children, but it was *Heidi*, which she wrote in 1881, which was her greatest success.
The heart-warming story of the little orphan girl who changes the lives of everyone she meets has delighted children for more than a hundred years.

One sunny June morning, a small girl climbs a steep mountain path to live with her grandfather. At first he is not pleased by her arrival, but soon he, like everyone else in the little mountain community, comes to love her. Heidi quickly adapts to the simple life her grandfather leads, and grows to love the mountains and scenery around her. But one day, her Aunt Dete comes to take her away to live in the city with Clara, a little invalid girl, and the fierce Fraulein Rottenmeier. Although dreadfully unhappy at leaving her beautiful mountain home, Heidi brings sunshine and happiness to her drab city surroundings. Her warmth and kindness endear her to everyone she meets, until at last she is able to return home to her grandfather.

This edition of *Heidi* has been lightly abridged and charmingly illustrated. Young readers will be enchanted.

# Contents

# 1

# Up the mountain to Alm-Uncle

ON A clear, sunny morning in June, a strong-looking girl and a small child climbed up the narrow mountain path from the village of Mayenfield in the Swiss Alps. After an hour, they came to the little hamlet of Dorfli, halfway up the mountain, where the girl had once lived.

"Are you tired, Heidi?" asked the girl.

"No, but I'm hot," answered the child. This was not surprising since she was wearing several layers of clothing.

They were passing the last of the houses when a woman came out of a door. Her name was Barbel. "Wait, Dete," she said to the girl. "I'll come with you."

And she joined the other two.

"Is this your sister's child?" she asked.

"Yes," replied Dete. "I'm taking her to stay with Uncle."

"Stay with Alm-Uncle!" cried Barbel. "He'll soon send you packing!"

"He's her grandfather and it's his duty," said Dete. "I've looked after Heidi since my sister died, but now I've the chance of a good job with a family in Frankfurt."

"The old man has nothing to do with anybody," said Barbel. "When he comes to the village, everybody stays out of his way."

Dete looked round, but the child had wandered off. "Where is she?"

"She's climbing up the slope with Peter, the goat-herd," said Barbel, pointing away from the footpath. "She'll be all right. Tell me about Alm-Uncle. Was he ever a rich man?"

"He once owned a large farm," replied Dete, "but he drank and gambled away the whole of his property. His parents died of broken hearts when they found out."

"Goodness!" said Barbel.

"He went to Naples as a soldier and nothing was heard of him for twelve or fifteen years," Dete went on. "Then he came to live in Dorfli with his little boy. The boy's name was Tobias and everybody liked him. Tobias grew up and got work as a carpenter. Then he married a girl from the village – my sister, Adelaide. They had a little girl – Heidi."

"What happened to Tobias?" asked Barbel.

"There was an accident," said Dete. "A wooden beam fell on him when he was working. He was killed on the spot. Adelaide never got over the shock. She developed a fever and died just two months later. People said it was punishment for Uncle's godless way of life, and some told him! After that he wouldn't speak to anybody and he went to live up the Alm mountain. Heidi came to live with me. I found work – sewing and knitting – but now a family I work for has asked me to go to Frankfurt with them. It's a good chance for me,

but I can't take a child who is five years old."

They had come to the small, ramshackle cottage where Peter, the goat-herd, lived with his mother and grandmother. Peter was eleven. Every day he took his goats up the mountain where they grazed on the delicious mountain plants until evening, when he brought them down again.

"I'll leave you here," Barbel told Dete. "I want to have a word with Peter's grandmother. Goodbye, Dete, and good luck!"

Dete walked on, looking for Heidi and Peter and the goats.

Peter often led the flock away from the path. Heidi was struggling after him, hot under her layers of clothes. She looked enviously at Peter, who was wearing just his short trousers. All at once, Heidi sat down and pulled off her shoes and stockings, threw off her hot red shawl and undid her frock. It was off in a second, but there was another one under it. (Dete had put Heidi's Sunday frock over her everyday one to save carrying it.) Heidi took off the second frock and wearing just her petticoat, stretched out her bare arms with glee. She left her little heap of clothes and bounded happily after Peter.

Some minutes later, Dete caught up with them.

"Heidi!" she cried. "Where are all your clothes?"

Heidi pointed to the heap, further down the mountain.

"You naughty girl!" said Dete. "Peter, go and fetch them for me."

Peter ran down and was back in a minute, carrying the clothes.

"You can carry them up to Uncle's for me," said Dete.

After forty minutes they reached Alm-Uncle's hut. It stood on a rock above the valley. Behind it were three fir trees and beyond these rose another mountain. The lower part was covered with beautiful grass and plants. The old man sat on a bench seat outside the hut, smoking his pipe. He looked up as the children, the goats and Dete clambered into view.

Heidi ran straight up to him. "Good-day, Grandfather," she said.

The old man scowled. "What's the meaning of this?" he said.

"Good-day, Uncle," said Dete. "I've brought you Tobias' and Adelaide's child. You'll hardly recognise her, as you've not seen her since she was a year old."

"And what's she to do with me?" said the old man. Then he called out to Peter. "You! Be off with your goats and take mine with you!"

Peter quickly obeyed.

"The child is to stay with you," Dete told the old man. "I've done my duty these last four years. Now it's time for you to do yours."

"What if the child is unhappy and cries for you?" said the old man.

"That's your affair," said Dete. "You'll be responsible if any harm comes to her. I'd have thought you already had enough on your conscience."

"Go back to where you came from!" he shouted. "And don't let me see your face again!"

Dete did not wait to be told twice. "Goodbye, Heidi," she called, and she hurried off down the mountain.

# 2

# At home with Grandfather

WHEN DETE was gone, the old man sat and stared at the ground, thick curls of smoke floating up from his pipe. Heidi explored her new surroundings. She found a shed where the goats were kept. It was empty now. She listened to the breeze blowing and whispering through the branches of the fir trees, then she went back to where her grandfather was sitting.

"What do you want?" he said.

"I want to see what you have inside the house," said Heidi.

"Come on then, and bring your bundle of clothes with you," he said.

"I won't need them any more," said Heidi.

"Well, bring them in. We must put them in the cupboard."

There was one room on the ground floor of the hut. It had a table and a chair in the centre and Grandfather's bed in one corner. In another corner was the hearth with a kettle hanging above it. On the other side of the room was a large wall cupboard. Grandfather opened it. Inside were his clothes, some plates, cups and glasses. On a higher shelf was a round loaf, some smoked meat and some cheese.

Heidi put her clothes in the cupboard. "Where do I sleep?"

"Wherever you like," Grandfather answered.

Heidi climbed a short ladder against the wall near her grandfather's bed. She found herself in the hay-loft. There was a heap of sweet-smelling hay and a little round window where she could see the valley.

"I'll sleep here, Grandfather," she said.

And she made a little bed for herself with hay. Grandfather brought her up a long piece of coarse brown stuff for a sheet, and she put down an extra layer of hay for a pillow. "We need a cover now," she said.

So the old man climbed back down the ladder, fetched a large, thick sack, then helped her spread it over the bed.

"It's a lovely bed!" said Heidi, delighted.

Grandfather sat down on a three-legged stool and toasted a large piece of cheese over the fire. While he did this, Heidi put the round loaf, two plates and two knives on the table.

"I'm glad you can think for yourself," said Grandfather, putting the toasted cheese and a jug of milk on the table. "What will you sit on?"

Heidi ran and got the three-legged stool.

"It's too low, but it will do for the moment," said the old man.

Heidi fetched a bowl and a glass from the cupboard and Grandfather filled the bowl with milk from the jug. Heidi was thirsty after her journey and she drank without stopping.

"Was that nice?" asked Grandfather.

11

"Yes!" said Heidi. Grandfather filled her bowl again.

When they had finished their meal, Grandfather went outside to the goat-shed. He found some long sticks and a flat, round board, in which he made some holes. Next he stuck the sticks into them – and there was a three-legged stool, just like his own but higher!

"It's a stool for me!" said Heidi, surprised and delighted.

When evening came, the goats came down from the mountain with Peter. Heidi ran to meet them. Two of the goats – one white and one brown – ran to the old man, for he was holding some salt which he always had ready for them when they returned home.

Peter went on with the rest of his flock while Heidi stroked the two goats in turn. Grandfather told her to fetch her bowl and some bread. When she came back, he milked the white goat and filled her bowl.

"Now eat your supper," he said, breaking off a piece of bread. "I must go and shut up the goats."

"What are their names, Grandfather?" asked Heidi.

"The white one is Little Swan, and the brown one is Little Bear."

Heidi called goodnight to the goats, then finished her supper and went inside. She put on her nightdress and climbed up the ladder to her bed of hay. Within minutes, she was fast asleep.

# 3

# Out with the goats

HEIDI WAS awakened next morning by a loud whistle. It was Peter with his flock of goats. She quickly jumped out of bed, put on her clothes and ran outside. Grandfather was bringing out Little Swan and Little Bear.

"Do you want to go with them up the mountain?" he asked Heidi.

"Yes, please!" she cried excitedly.

"Then you must wash and make yourself tidy."

He pointed to a large tub of water beside the door and Heidi ran across and began splashing and rubbing. Grandfather took Peter inside the hut and gave him a large piece of bread, some cheese and a little bowl.

"Milk two bowlfuls from the goats for her dinner," he told the boy. "She can come back with you this evening, but take care of her."

The children began their climb a few minutes later. The sun shone down on the green slopes and Heidi picked handfuls of little flowers. Peter was busy with the goats, who ran in all directions. He whistled and swung his stick to gather them together again.

They climbed to the place where Peter always stopped to let his goats graze. It was at the foot of the high rocks. The valley lay far below, bathed in the morning sun. Heidi sat and stared at everything. There was a great stillness, only broken by light puffs of wind. She drank in the sunlight, the fresh air, and the sweet smell of the flowers. She wished that she could stay there for ever.

After a while she got up and began to run among the goats, getting to know each of them. Peter took the bread and cheese from his bag and put them on the ground. Then he took the bowl and milked the white goat.

"Time for dinner!" he called to Heidi, and she skipped across to him.

"Is the milk for me?" she said.

"Yes," replied Peter, "and the two large pieces of bread and cheese are yours. And when you've drunk that milk, you're to have another bowlful from the white goat."

"Which goat do you get your milk from?" she asked.

"From my own goat," he said.

Heidi drank the milk, then broke off a piece of her bread. She held out the remainder, together with a big slice of cheese. "You can have that, Peter, I have plenty."

Peter was astonished at such generosity. "Thank you," he said.

"The prettiest goats are Little Swan and Little Bear," said Heidi.

"I know," said Peter. "Alm-Uncle brushes and washes them and gives them salt, and he has a nice shed for them."

Suddenly, he jumped up. One of the young goats had got too close to the

edge of the rocks and was about to fall over. Peter grabbed one of her hind legs just in time! The animal struggled to get loose, still dangerously close to the edge. Heidi quickly saw the danger. She snatched some sweet-smelling leaves and held them under the goat's nose. The young animal began to eat from Heidi's hand and was coaxed away from the edge. Peter could stand up and take hold of her collar. He led the animal back to a safe place on the mountain.

The afternoon passed, and the sun was about to drop out of sight behind the mountains. Heidi suddenly noticed how the rocks above were beginning to shine and glow. She sprang to her feet.

"Peter!" she cried. "Everything is on fire! The rocks, the great snow mountain and the sky!"

"It's always like that," said Peter. "But it's not really fire."

"How beautiful!" said Heidi. "Oh, but now all the colour is dying away! It's all gone, Peter!"

"It will come again tomorrow," he told her. "But we must go home." And he whistled his goats together.

# 4

# Peter's Grandmother

EACH MORNING during that summer, Heidi went up the mountain with Peter and the goats. She became strong, healthy and brown from the sun. Then the warm, bright sun disappeared and it got much colder. One night there was a heavy fall of snow which covered everything and there was no Peter the next day. Heidi watched as the thick snowflakes fell and the snow piled so high that they couldn't open the door. Then it stopped, and Grandfather shovelled it away from the house.

One afternoon, a week later, Peter came.

"Well, Peter," said the old man. "How is school going?" He turned to Heidi and explained. "Peter goes to school in the winter to learn how to read and write. It's a bit hard, isn't it, Peter?"

"Yes, it is," agreed Peter.

Heidi asked lots of questions about school. Then they all had supper before it was time for Peter to go home.

"Grandmother said she would like to see you," he told Heidi.

Heidi liked the idea of visiting, but it was another four days before Grandfather thought it was safe enough to go. By then the snow was as hard as ice and the ground crackled underfoot. Grandfather got a large sledge from the shed. There was a seat inside it and a pole at the side to guide the vehicle. He wrapped Heidi up in a warm sack and sat her on his lap. He grasped the pole with his right hand and pushed the sledge forward with his feet. It shot down the mountain so fast that Heidi thought they were flying! She shouted with delight.

They came to a standstill outside Peter's home and Grandfather lifted Heidi out. "You can go in," he said, "but come home when it begins to get dark." And he set off up the mountain, pulling the sledge behind him.

Heidi opened the door and found herself in a tiny, dark kitchen. She went through into another small room. This was not a hut like her Grandfather's with one large room and hay-loft. Instead it was an old cottage. Peter's mother was sitting at a table, mending a waistcoat. In the corner, an old woman sat spinning. Heidi went across and put out her hand.

"Good-day, Grandmother," she said.

The old woman lifted her head and felt for the hand that the child held out to her. "Are you Heidi?" she said.

"Yes," said Heidi. "I came down on the sledge with Grandfather."

"Is it possible? Did Alm-Uncle really bring you down? Perhaps what Peter has been telling us about him is true. What is the child like, Brigitta?" she asked Peter's mother.

"She is like Adelaide. Her eyes are dark and her hair is curly, like her

father's and the old man's," said Brigitta.

Heidi looked round the room. "Look, Grandmother, one of your window shutters is flapping backwards and forwards."

"Ah, child, I can't see it," said the old woman. "But everything in the cottage rattles and creaks when the wind is blowing. The house is falling to pieces and there's no one to mend it. Peter can't do it. Some nights I lie awake waiting for it to fall down around us."

"Why can't you see the shutter, Grandmother?" said Heidi. "Perhaps if you went outside in the white snow where there is more light – "

"It's always dark for me, child, whether there's snow or sun."

"Can't you see the mountains catch fire when the sun goes down?"

"No, child, I'll never see the mountains on fire again," said the old woman sadly.

Heidi began to cry. "Can no one make it light for you?" she sobbed.

The old woman tried to comfort Heidi. "Come here, my dear, and tell me about your Grandfather. I knew him very well in the old days."

So Heidi talked of her life with Grandfather – how he had made her a stool and a new milk bowl and spoon out of wood. And she told of the days she had spent on the mountain with Peter and the goats.

The old woman listened with great interest. "Do you hear this, Brigitta?" she said. "Alm-Uncle is kind to the child."

The conversation was interrupted by Peter marching in.

"Back from school already?" said his grandmother. "How's the reading getting on, Peter?"

"Just the same," said Peter.

The old woman sighed. "I was hoping he'd have learned to read that book," she told Heidi, pointing to a book on a shelf. "It's an old prayer-book with beautiful songs, but I can't remember them any more."

The afternoon had grown darker and Heidi realised it was time for her to leave. "I must go home now, Grandmother," she said.

"Wait," said the old woman. "Peter must go with you. Do you have something warm to put on?"

But Heidi was already outside. Her Grandfather had come to meet her. He wrapped her up in the sack and lifted her into his arms. Then he strode off up the mountain. Brigitta and Peter watched them, then ran inside to tell the old woman.

As soon as they were home, Heidi told Grandfather about Peter's cottage. "It rattles and shakes in the wind," she said. "We must go back tomorrow with a hammer and some nails and mend it."

"We must, must we?" he said. "Who told you that?"

"Nobody told me," said Heidi. "But Peter's grandmother lies awake at night, afraid that it's going to fall down on them. We must help her."

Grandfather looked at her for some time without speaking. Then he said, "Yes, Heidi, we must do something. We'll go tomorrow."

And the following morning, they went down to Peter's cottage. While Heidi talked to Peter's grandmother, Grandfather mended the windows and the roof. Peter's mother tried to thank him for his kindness, but he stopped her. "I know what you all think of me without your telling me," he said.

And so the Winter went by. But Peter's blind grandmother had found someone to make her happy. Each fine Winter's day Heidi came down on Grandfather's sledge, and he often brought a hammer and nails with him. The cottage no longer groaned and rattled and Peter's grandmother was able to sleep in peace. She said she would never forget what Alm-Uncle had done for her.

# 5

# Two visitors

A YEAR passed quickly, and soon another Winter was almost over. Heidi was now eight years old. Little Swan and Little Bear followed her everywhere and gave a bleat of pleasure when they heard her voice. Twice during the Winter Peter brought a message from the school at Dorfli, telling Grandfather to send Heidi there. But each time Grandfather replied that he did not intend to send Heidi to school. Then one March morning, when the snows had melted and Heidi was running around outside, an old gentleman dressed in black arrived at the hut.

"You must be Heidi," he said. "Where is your grandfather?"

He was the old village pastor from Dorfli. He had once been a neighbour of Grandfather's when the old man had lived in the village.

"Grandfather is inside," said Heidi.

The pastor went into the hut.

"Good morning," he said to Grandfather. "It's a long time since I've seen you, neighbour."

Grandfather looked surprised but pushed a chair towards the other man. "Sit down," he said.

"I expect you know why I'm here," said the pastor. He nodded towards the window where they could see Heidi outside. "The child ought to have been at school a year ago."

"I'm not sending her to school," said Grandfather. "I'm going to let her grow up and be happy among the goats and birds. She's safe with them and will learn nothing evil."

"But the child is not a goat or a bird! This is the last Winter she must be allowed to run wild. Next Winter she must come to school."

"No!" replied Grandfather. "I'll not send her down the mountain on ice-cold mornings, nor let her return at night when the wind is raging."

"Then why not do what you ought to have done long ago?" said the pastor. "Come and live in the village. What sort of life is this? If anything were to happen to you, who could help you?"

"I know you mean well," said Grandfather, "but I'll not send the child to school. Nor will I come and live in the village."

"Then God help you," said the pastor. And he turned sadly away and went down the mountain.

Grandfather was silent for the rest of that day and the following morning. But soon after dinner, another visitor arrived. It was Dete.

She wore a fine feathered hat and a long trailing skirt. "I've come to take Heidi," she told Grandfather. "Some rich friends of the lady I work for have a daughter who has to go about in a wheelchair. Her father wants a companion

for her and the lady-housekeeper has described the sort of child they want –
simple, unspoiled and not like city children. I thought at once of Heidi and
I've agreed to take her there. It's a wonderful opportunity. The people are very
rich. And who can tell? If they like Heidi, they may – "

"Have you nearly finished?" interrupted Grandfather. "Because I'll have
nothing to do with it."

Dete became angry. "Listen! The child is eight years old and knows
nothing. You won't send her to church or school. She's my sister's child and
I'm responsible for her. I'm not going to give in and I have everybody in Dorfli
on my side. And I advise you to think carefully before fighting this in court.
There are things that could be brought up against you that you wouldn't wish
to have raked up again."

"Silence!" thundered the old man. "Go! And never let me see you or your
feathered hats again!" And with that he strode out of the hut.

"You've made Grandfather angry," said Heidi, scowling at Dete.

"He'll soon get over it. Show me where your clothes are."

"I'm not coming," said Heidi.

"Don't be stupid! Didn't you hear your Grandfather? He doesn't want to see
us again. He wants you to come with me, not make him angrier still. It's nice
in Frankfurt and if you don't like it, you can come back when he's in a better
temper."

"Can I come back this evening?" said Heidi.

"I've told you that you can come back when you like," said Dete. She
bundled Heidi's clothes together and hurried the child out of the hut and down
the mountain before Grandfather came back.

As they passed Peter's cottage, they saw the boy working outside.

"Where are you going, Heidi?" he called.

"To Frankfurt," said Heidi. She turned to Dete. "I must say goodbye to
Grandmother – "

"There's no time for that," said Dete, pulling her on past the cottage. "You
can go and see her when you come back."

Peter ran into the cottage with the news that Dete was taking Heidi to
Frankfurt. His grandmother was very upset. She opened the window and
shouted, "Dete! Dete! Don't take the child away from us."

But although Dete heard her, she didn't stop.

23

# 6

# Frankfurt and Clara

IN HER home in Frankfurt, Clara, the little daughter of Herr Sesemann, was lying on the couch in the study. Her face was thin and pale.

"Isn't it time yet, Fraulein Rottenmeier?" she asked.

Fraulein Rottenmeier sat at her work-table, busy with her embroidery. She was the housekeeper and was in charge of the servants whenever Herr Sesemann was away. But before she could reply, a coach arrived at the front door and Dete and Heidi stepped out. A few minutes later, Sebastian, one of the servants, brought them into the study.

Fraulein Rottenmeier rose slowly and walked over to them.

"What is your name, child?" she asked Heidi.

"Heidi," came the answer.

"That's no name for a child!" said Fraulein Rottenmeier. "What name were you given?"

"I don't remember," said Heidi.

"Her name is Adelaide," Dete said quickly. "She was named after her mother, my sister."

"What age is she?" said Fraulein Rottenmeier. "I didn't expect to see so young a child. Clara is twelve, and I wanted a companion of a similar age to share her lessons."

"I – I'm not certain how old she is now," said Dete. "Perhaps ten – "

"Grandfather says I'm eight," said Heidi.

"Only eight!" said Fraulein Rottenmeier. "What books do you have for your lessons?"

"None," said Heidi. "I can't read."

"Can't read!" said Fraulein Rottenmeier. She turned to Dete. "Young woman, this is not the sort of child you led me to expect."

"Excuse me," said Dete, "but the child is exactly what I thought you required. A simple girl, unlike other children. But I must go now, my mistress will be waiting for me." And before the other woman could reply, Dete ran from the room.

For a moment, Fraulein Rottenmeier was too taken aback to move, but then she hurried after Dete, leaving Heidi in the room.

Clara had been watching and listening, but now she beckoned to Heidi. "Come here," she said. "Would you rather be called Adelaide or Heidi?"

"I'm never called anything but Heidi," said Heidi.

"Then that's what I'll call you," said Clara. "Are you pleased to come to Frankfurt?"

"No," said Heidi. "But I'll go home again tomorrow and take Grandmother a white loaf."

"You are a funny child!" laughed Clara. "You were meant to share my lessons, but you can't even read. There will be some fun with my tutor when he comes!"

Fraulein Rottenmeier came back into the room. She had not been able to catch Dete and was annoyed. Now it was time for dinner and Sebastian came to push Clara's chair into the dining room. Heidi went with them.

There were three places laid at the table, and beside Heidi's plate was a nice white roll. "Can I have this?" she whispered to Sebastian, who nodded. Heidi immediately seized the roll and put it into her pocket.

Fraulein Rottenmeier had not noticed. She began to tell Heidi all the things she must do and how she must behave if she was going to stay with them. But it had been a long day for Heidi, and the little girl was asleep long before Fraulein Rottenmeier had finished.

# 7

# Seven kittens

WHEN HEIDI opened her eyes on her first morning in Frankfurt she could not think where she was. She was in a high, white bed in a very large room. There was a washstand in the corner, and near the window were two large chairs and a sofa, both with flower-patterned covers.

Heidi jumped out of bed and ran to the window. She wanted to see the sky and the country, but the window was too high to look out of properly. She could see nothing but the walls and windows of other buildings.

Clara was already at breakfast by the time Heidi came down. After the meal, Heidi followed Sebastian as he wheeled Clara to the study.

Fraulein Rottenmeier saw the tutor first and explained that Heidi did not know her ABC and could not read. As they walked to the study they heard a loud crash. Fraulein Rottenmeier rushed in to see a heap of exercise books, an ink-stand and a tablecloth, on the floor. A stream of ink was running into the carpet. "Whatever – !" she began.

Clara was giggling. "Heidi did it. Several carriages were passing the house and she jumped up to run and see what the sound was. By accident she dragged the tablecloth with her as she got up."

Fraulein Rottenmeier ran from the room to the top of the stairs. There, standing in the open doorway at the bottom, was Heidi, looking into the street with amazement.

"What are you doing?" Fraulein Rottenmeier called down to her.

"I thought I heard the sound of fir trees blowing in the wind," said Heidi, "but I can't hear them any more."

"It was the sound of carriages passing, you stupid girl!" said Fraulein Rottenmeier. "Fir trees! What a ridiculous idea! Come back upstairs and see the mess you've made."

Heidi was surprised. She had been in such a hurry to investigate the fir-tree sound that she hadn't noticed what she had done.

"You must sit still during your lessons," Fraulein Rottenmeier told her, "or I'll tie you to the chair. Do you understand?"

"Yes," replied Heidi.

But there was little opportunity for lessons that morning by the time Sebastian had cleared up the mess in the study. In the afternoon Clara went to rest on her bed.

Heidi spoke to Sebastian. "There's nothing outside but stony streets," she said. "Where can I go to see over the whole valley?"

"You'd have to climb to the top of a church tower, like that one there," he said, pointing out of the window at a church.

A few moments later, Heidi went out of the door and into the street. But the

tower was not as near as it had looked from the window. She went down the street and round several corners, but she was still no closer to it. There were people passing by, but they all seemed in such a hurry that Heidi did not like to ask them the way to go.

Then she came to a corner where a boy was standing. He carried a hand-organ and there was a monkey on his shoulder.

"How can I get to the church with the tall tower?" she asked him.

"What will you give me if I take you?" he said. "Money?"

"I haven't got any," said Heidi, "but Clara has, and I'm sure she'll give you some. How much do you want?"

"Twopence," he said.

"Come along then," said Heidi.

The boy took her through the streets to the church and an old man answered the church door when they knocked.

"What do you want?" said the old man crossly.

"I want to go up the tower," said Heidi. "Please!"

The old man saw how anxious she was. "Well, if you really want to go up, I'll take you," he said.

The boy sat down to wait outside and Heidi took the old man's hand as he led her up to the tower. It was a long climb. When they reached the top, the man lifted Heidi up so that she could look out of the open window. There, beneath them, was a sea of roofs, towers and chimney pots.

"It's not what I expected," said Heidi, disappointed.

They began to go back down again and passed the tower-keeper's room. Inside was a large cat and a basket of seven kittens.

Heidi ran in to look at them. "Oh, the sweet little things!"

"Would you like them?" said the man.

Heidi almost jumped for joy. There would be plenty of room for them in the large house, and what a lovely surprise it would be for Clara.

"But how can I carry them?" asked Heidi.

"I'll bring them to you," he said. "Where do you live?"

"Herr Sesemann's house," said Heidi.

"I know it," said the man. "I'll bring them later."

The boy took Heidi back to the house and Sebastian opened the door.

"Hurry, Miss!" said Sebastian, pulling Heidi inside and slamming the door in the boy's face. "Fraulein Rottenmeier has been looking for you."

Suddenly, the front door bell began to ring loudly. Sebastian opened the door and saw the boy with the monkey. At the same moment, Fraulein Rottenmeier came to see what the noise was about.

"I want to see Clara!" the boy said. "I want my twopence!"

"Go away, you rascal!" said Sebastian. "Who told you to come here?"

"She did!" said the boy, pointing at Heidi.

Eventually, all was explained. Clara gave the boy twopence, but not before hearing some of the sweet music from his hand-organ. Then soon after, there was another surprise for her. The old man from the church arrived with the basket of kittens.

"For me?" said Clara, delighted.

And the kittens jumped out of the basket and began running all around the sitting room. Fraulein Rottenmeier was horrified, and climbed up on a chair out of the way. Sebastian quickly gathered up the animals and put them back in their basket while Clara and Heidi laughed and laughed.

# 8

# Herr Sesemann

HEIDI WENT to her lessons each day, but she did not learn to read. It was as difficult as Peter had said it was, she decided. And she was so homesick for Grandfather and the hut on the mountain that one day she made up her mind to go back. After all, Dete had told her she could go home whenever she liked. So she gathered up all the white rolls she had saved for Peter's grandmother and tied them into a shawl. Then she put on her straw hat and went downstairs.

"Where do you think you're going?" Fraulein Rottenmeier asked when she saw Heidi going down the steps outside the house.

"I'm going home," said Heidi, frightened by the fierce woman.

"And what would Herr Sesemann say if he knew you were running away?" said Fraulein Rottenmeier. "You ungrateful little thing! Have you ever been so well off and comfortable in your life?"

"But I can't see the sun say goodnight to the mountains here," said Heidi. "And Peter's grandmother needs her white bread, and – "

"Have mercy on us!" cried Fraulein Rottenmeier. "The child's lost her mind! Sebastian, bring her back in at once."

Sebastian did as he was told and took Heidi back to her room, trying to comfort her. "Don't let her make you unhappy," he said. "Keep your spirits up! We'll go and see the kittens later, shall we?"

Then a day or two later, Fraulein Rottenmeier discovered the heap of white rolls in Heidi's wardrobe. "What are these!" she cried.

"They're for Peter's grandmother," said Heidi. "Please leave them!"

But Fraulein Rottenmeier ordered Sebastian to throw the rolls away and poor Heidi ran down to Clara, sobbing.

"Now all Grandmother's bread has gone!" she cried.

Clara was upset to see Heidi like this. "Don't cry," she said. "You can have as many rolls as you want when you go home. Yours would have been hard and stale by then. Please don't cry, Heidi! Tell me more stories about Grandfather's hut, and about Peter and the goats."

And, at last, Heidi *did* stop crying.

But she did not stop wishing that she could go home.

A few days after this, Herr Sesemann returned home from Paris. It was late afternoon and he hurried to see his daughter before doing anything else. Heidi was sitting beside her.

Father and daughter greeted each other warmly. Then Herr Sesemann said, "So this is our little Swiss girl."

"Yes, this is Heidi," said Clara.

"Are you both good friends, or do you quarrel?" asked her father.

"Clara is always kind to me," said Heidi.

"And Heidi has never tried to quarrel," said Clara.

"I'm glad to hear it," said Herr Sesemann.

Fraulein Rottenmeier was waiting for him in the dining room and quickly told him how unhappy she was about Heidi. "If you only knew the things the girl has done, the kind of people and animals she has brought to the house, Herr Sesemann. Her behaviour is most peculiar. At times it seems as if she's not in her right mind."

After dinner, Herr Sesemann went to talk with his daughter again.

"Tell me about Heidi," he said to her, "and about the animals, and why Fraulein Rottenmeier thinks Heidi's not in her right mind sometimes."

Clara laughed and she told him about the bread rolls, about the kittens and about the boy with the hand-organ and the monkey. Her father laughed with her when he heard all this.

"So you don't want me to send the child home again?" he said.

"Oh, no!" said Clara. "It used to be so dull, but something fresh happens every day now and she tells me stories about the mountain."

That evening, Herr Sesemann informed Fraulein Rottenmeier that Heidi was to stay. "The child must be treated kindly," he said, "and her peculiarities must not be looked upon as crimes. My mother is coming to stay shortly and she'll help. She can get along with anybody."

# q

# An unhappy time

HERR SESEMANN went back to Paris after two weeks, but Clara's grandmother arrived a few days later. She had beautiful white hair and was an alert old lady, with all her wits about her. She knew what was happening in the house as soon as she entered it.

One afternoon when Clara was asleep on the couch, Frau Sesemann asked Fraulein Rottenmeier to bring Heidi to her room. "She's bored and lonely," she told the housekeeper. "I've some books I'd like to give her."

"She can't read," said Fraulein Rottenmeier. "The tutor's tried to teach her, but she seems to find it impossible."

"How strange," said the old lady. "But she can look at the pictures."

When Heidi came, she gazed in delight at the beautiful pictures in the books. But as she stared at one page, tears came into her eyes. The picture showed young animals grazing in a field and the sun sinking below the horizon. Frau Sesemann put a hand on Heidi's shoulder.

"Don't cry," she said in a kindly voice. "I expect the picture has reminded you of something, but there's a beautiful story with it which I'll read to you later. Now, how are you getting on with your lessons? Have you learned a lot?"

"Oh, no!" replied Heidi. "But I knew I wouldn't learn to read. Peter told me it was too difficult because he had tried."

"You must not always go by what Peter says, whoever he is. You must try for yourself. I'm certain you didn't give all your attention to the tutor, but now you'll try and you'll soon learn to read. And when you do, you can have that book to keep."

"Oh!" said Heidi. "If only I could read now!"

In spite of the kindness shown to her, Heidi still wanted to go home. But she didn't want to seem ungrateful to Herr Sesemann, or to upset Clara and her grandmother, so she said nothing to anyone. But often at night she lay awake thinking of Grandfather and the mountain. Her dreams were filled with snow-fields turning crimson in the evening light. And when she awoke, she would cry quietly into her pillow.

Her unhappiness did not escape Frau Sesemann. She noticed that the child ate very little and was becoming thin and pale.

"What's the matter, Heidi?" she asked. "Are you in trouble?"

"I can't tell you," replied Heidi.

"Can you tell Clara?"

"Oh, no! I can't tell anyone," said Heidi.

"Then this is what you must do," said Frau Sesemann. "Whenever we're in great trouble and can't speak to anyone about it, we must turn to God and pray for help. He can give the help that no one else can give."

"Can I tell Him everything?" said Heidi.

"Everything."

So Heidi ran to her room, put her hands together and told God about everything that was making her sad. She begged Him to let her go home to Grandfather and the mountain.

It was about a week after this that the tutor came to see Frau Sesemann.

"A most surprising thing has happened," he told her.

"Has Heidi learned to read?" said Frau Sesemann.

"Yes! How did you know?"

"Many unlikely things happen in this life," said Frau Sesemann, with a twinkle in her eye.

After the tutor had gone, Frau Sesemann went downstairs and found Heidi sitting beside Clara, reading aloud to her. And that evening, Heidi found the large book with the beautiful pictures lying beside her place at dinner. She looked up at Frau Sesemann.

"Is it really mine now?" she asked.

Frau Sesemann smiled. "Yes, it's yours now."

"For always? Even when I go home?"

"Yours for ever. Tomorrow we'll begin to read it."

Every afternoon when Clara was asleep, Frau Sesemann called Heidi to her room. She taught the child how to sew and make beautiful dolls' clothes and she listened as Heidi read aloud. But she noticed that the child never looked really happy.

"Are you still troubled, Heidi?" said Frau Sesemann. It was the last week of her visit and Heidi had just finished reading to her.

Heidi nodded.

"Have you told God about it?"

"Yes, but I've stopped praying," said Heidi. "God doesn't listen. I've prayed every day for weeks, but God hasn't done what I asked."

"God knows better than we do what is good for us," said Frau Sesemann. "If we ask Him for something that isn't good for us, He doesn't give it, but He gives something better. You must go on praying and trusting in Him."

Frau Sesemann's words went straight to Heidi's heart. "I'll ask God to forgive me," said Heidi, "and I'll never forget Him again."

The house seemed silent and empty after Frau Sesemann went. Heidi began to read to Clara from her book, but she had hardly begun a story about a dying grandmother before she cried out, "Oh, perhaps Peter's grandmother is dead!" And she burst into tears.

Clara tried to explain that the story was about a quite different grandmother. But although Heidi knew this, she wept even more loudly because it came to her that Peter's grandmother, and even her grandfather, might die before she could get home to see them again.

Fraulein Rottenmeier came into the room and Clara explained what had happened. "Now, stop crying!" Fraulein Rottenmeier told Heidi. "If there are any more scenes like this I'll take that book away from you."

Heidi turned white with fear. The book was her one great treasure. She quickly dried her tears and never cried again when she was reading. But she lost her appetite and became pale and thin again. At night she would remember her home and would weep into her pillow.

# 10

# The midnight ghost

ONE MORNING, Sebastian came down and found the front door wide open. And on the following two mornings, either Sebastian or one of the other servants found it wide open for no apparent reason. At first they thought a thief had got in, but nothing was missing from the house.

Finally, after a great deal of persuasion from Fraulein Rottenmeier, Sebastian and John, another of the servants, agreed to sit up one night and see what happened. But both of them fell asleep before midnight.

Then, as the clock struck midnight, Sebastian roused himself. Everything was still and there was no sound from the streets outside. Sebastian was too nervous to go to sleep again and he shook John gently to wake him up. John stood up and, sounding braver than he felt, said, "We must go outside and see what's going on. Don't be afraid, Sebastian, just follow me." He opened the hall door – and a gust of wind blew out the light in his hand.

John was already pushing Sebastian back into the other room.

"What's the matter?" said Sebastian. "What did you see?"

"The door partly open," gasped John, "and a white figure standing at the top of the steps!"

Sebastian felt his blood run cold. The two sat down close to one another and did not move again until it was light and the streets were bustling with people and traffic.

When Fraulein Rottenmeier heard about this ghostly experience, she wrote to Herr Sesemann, telling him that he must come home because of the mysterious happenings in his house and because Clara might be in danger. Herr Sesemann was very surprised to receive such a letter but, concerned for his daughter, he immediately returned to Frankfurt.

"Have you or any of the other servants been playing tricks, Sebastian?" he asked his servant.

"No, sir!" said Sebastian. "On our honour!"

"Then you must take a message to my old friend the doctor. Give him my kind regards and ask him to come tonight at nine o'clock. Tell him to be prepared to spend the night here."

The doctor was a silver-haired man with kindly eyes and an anxious expression on his face. "Is someone ill?" he asked, when he arrived that evening.

"Much worse than that, doctor," said Herr Sesemann. "There's a ghost in the house. My house is haunted!"

The doctor laughed loudly, but Herr Sesemann told him how the front door of the house was mysteriously opened each night. Then he gave him a loaded revolver and kept one himself so that they were prepared for anything that happened.

The two men waited in the same room where Sebastian and John had kept watch. A bottle of wine was on the table and the two revolvers lay beside it. Two good-sized lamps had also been lit, for Herr Sesemann was determined not to wait for any ghosts in half-darkness.

One o'clock struck and everything was quiet.

Suddenly, the doctor lifted a finger.

"Sesemann, do you hear something?" he whispered.

They both listened – *and heard a key being turned and a door being opened.* Herr Sesemann put out his hand for his revolver and picked up one of the lights. The doctor did the same and the two men crept out into the hall.

Moonlight streamed through the open front door and fell on a white figure standing motionless in the doorway.

"Who's there?" thundered the doctor, in a voice that echoed through the hall.

The figure turned and gave a cry. There, in her little white nightgown, stood Heidi. She was staring wild-eyed at the lights and revolvers and trembling all over.

"It's your little Swiss girl, Sesemann!" said the doctor.

"Child, what does this mean," said Herr Sesemann. "Why did you come down here?"

White with terror and hardly able to speak, Heidi answered, "I – I don't know."

But now the doctor stepped forward. "This is a matter for me, Sesemann," he said. And he carried Heidi up to her bedroom and laid her on her bed. Gradually, she became calmer and stopped trembling.

The doctor held her hand. "Now tell me, where were you wanting to go?" he said. "Had you been dreaming?"

"Yes," said Heidi, "I dream the same dream every night. I'm back with Grandfather and I hear the sound in the fir trees outside and I see the stars shining. Then I open the door quickly and run out and it's all so beautiful. But when I wake up, I'm still in Frankfurt."

"Are you happy here in Frankfurt?" asked the doctor.

"Yes," came the quiet reply, but it sounded more like "No".

"And where did you live with your grandfather?"

"Up on the mountain," answered Heidi.

"Wasn't that rather dull at times?"

"No, no, it was beautiful!" said Heidi. And she began to cry as she remembered all the things she was missing.

The doctor stood up. "There, there, go to sleep now. Tomorrow everything will be all right, you'll see."

He went downstairs and spoke with Herr Sesemann.

"The child is walking in her sleep because she's unhappy," he said. "She's so homesick that she's making herself ill. You must send her home, Sesemann. She must go tomorrow."

# 11

# On the mountain again

CLARA WAS upset when her father told her Heidi was going home. She made all sorts of suggestions for keeping Heidi with her, but her father was firm. He promised to take her to Switzerland the next summer if she made no further fuss. So Clara gave in, but asked if she could put some things in a box for Heidi.

The servants had been told what was happening, and Fraulein Rottenmeier was at first astonished and then a little disappointed when Herr Sesemann said nothing about ghostly visitors in the night.

Dete was sent for and was asked if she would take Heidi back to the mountain. Dete remembered Uncle's last words – that he never wished to set eyes on her again – and excused herself by saying that it was quite impossible for her to get time off from her work to take the child. Herr Sesemann quickly understood that she was unwilling to take Heidi at all and he sent her away.

He sent for Sebastian and told the young man that he was to travel with Heidi, then he wrote a letter for Heidi's grandfather.

A little later, when Heidi came to the dining room, Herr Sesemann said, "Well, what do you say to this, little one?"

Heidi gave him a puzzled look.

"I see you know nothing about it," he laughed. "You're going home today."

"Home?" Heidi turned pale and found it difficult to breathe.

"Don't you want to go?"

"Oh, yes, yes!" she cried.

Heidi was too excited to eat her breakfast, so Herr Sesemann instructed Sebastian to pack some food to take with them. Then he told Heidi to go and see Clara in her room.

Clara showed her the things she had put in a box – dresses, aprons and handkerchiefs. "And look here," said Clara, holding up a basket. Heidi peeped in and jumped for joy. Inside were twelve round white rolls for Peter's grandmother!

Then someone called, "The carriage is here!"

Heidi ran to her room to fetch her precious book, which was under her pillow, and put it in the basket with the rolls. Then she said her goodbyes to Clara and Herr Sesemann and climbed into the carriage with Sebastian.

"Say goodbye and thank you to the doctor for me," she called back as the carriage pulled away.

They then took the train to Basle and stayed overnight in a hotel. The next day they took another train to Mayenfield and were going to walk to Dorfli from there.

Sebastian was not looking forward to the climb to Dorfli. He was not used to

mountains and was a little afraid of them. Outside the station was a man with a horse and cart. He was loading heavy sacks which had arrived on the train.

"Which is the safest way to Dorfli?" Sebastian asked him.

"All roads here are safe," came the reply. "I'm going to Dorfli myself. Do you want me to take that box?"

After some discussion, it was finally agreed that the man should take both Heidi and the box on his cart to Dorfli, which was a great relief to Sebastian. He gave Heidi the letter for her grandfather and a parcel which he said was a present from Herr Sesemann. Then he went back to the station platform to await a return train.

Heidi went as far as Dorfli in the cart, then began her walk up the mountain. "Grandfather will come for the box," she told the man on the cart.

Heidi climbed the steep path as quickly as she could. One thought filled her mind: was Peter's grandmother still alive? Then she caught sight of the cottage in the hollow of the mountain and her heart began to beat faster. She ran to the doorway, unable to make a sound.

"Dear God," came a voice from inside. "That is how Heidi used to run in. If only I could have her with me once again! Who is there?"

"It's me, Grandmother!" cried Heidi, and she ran and threw her arms around the old woman, unable to speak for joy.

The old woman put a hand on Heidi's head, and said, "Yes, yes, that's her hair and her voice! God has answered my prayers!"

"I've brought you some white rolls," said Heidi, taking them from the basket and piling them in the old woman's lap.

"Oh, what a blessing!" said Peter's grandmother. "But you're the greatest blessing of all, Heidi! Tell me everything you've been doing."

Heidi told her how unhappy she had been and how she had been afraid she would never see Grandmother or the mountain again. "But now I must go home to see Grandfather," she said eventually. "I'll come again tomorrow. Goodnight, Grandmother."

"Yes, please come again tomorrow," said the old woman.

Heidi continued her way up the mountain, her basket on her arm. All around were the steep, green slopes, bright in the evening sun. Suddenly a warm, red glow fell on everything and she saw the two mountain peaks above her, like two great flames. Tears of happiness came into Heidi's eyes and she thanked God for being home.

Now she ran on until the little hut came into view. And there was Grandfather, sitting on the bench seat as always, smoking his pipe.

"Grandfather! Grandfather!" she cried, and threw her arms around his neck.

The old man could not speak for some minutes. For the first time in many years his eyes were wet. Then he sat Heidi on his knee and said, "So you've come back to me. Did they send you away?"

"Oh, no, Grandfather," said Heidi. "You mustn't think that. They were all so kind – Clara and her father, and Frau Sesemann. But all I wanted was to come home to you, although I said nothing because it would have seemed ungrateful. Oh, and I have a letter and a parcel for you from Herr Sesemann."

Grandfather read the letter. There was some money – a lot of money – in the parcel. "That belongs to you," he told Heidi. "Now you can buy a bed and bedclothes and dresses."

"I'm sure I don't want it," said Heidi. "I've got a bed already, and Clara has put such a lot of clothes in my box I'll never need any more."

"Take it and put it in the cupboard. You'll want it some day."

Heidi skipped into the hut after her Grandfather. She was delighted to see everything again. "But where is my bed?" she said.

"We can soon make it up again," said Grandfather. "Now, come and have your milk."

She was drinking her milk when she heard a shrill whistle outside. It was Peter with the goats. Heidi ran out to them.

"Good evening, Peter," she said. "Little Swan! Little Bear! Do you know me again?" And the animals immediately began rubbing their heads against her, bleating with pleasure.

"So you're back," said Peter when he had got over his surprise. "I'm glad." And the two children smiled broadly at one another.

It was with a happy heart that Heidi lay down on her hay-bed that night, and she slept more soundly than she had for a year.

# A beautiful story
# for Grandfather

THE NEXT day was Saturday and Grandfather came down with Heidi to
Peter's cottage. He left her there and went on down to Dorfli to fetch her box.
Peter's grandmother was pleased to see Heidi again and told her how much
she had enjoyed the first of the white rolls. And Peter's mother said that she
was sure Grandmother would be stronger and healthier if she could always
have white rolls like that.

"The baker in Dorfli makes them, but they are much more expensive than
the black bread," she said.

Heidi had an idea. "I've got lots of money," she said. "You shall have a fresh
white roll every day and two on Sundays. Peter can bring them up from
Dorfli."

"No, no, child!" said the old lady. "I can't let you spend your money like that.
You must give it to your grandfather and he'll tell you how you can spend it."

But Heidi would not be put off and was determined that Peter's
grandmother should have her white rolls. Then she caught sight of the old
song book and had another idea.

"Grandmother, I can read now," she said. "Shall I read one of the hymns
from your book?"

"Oh, yes! Can you really read, child?"

So Heidi read a song from the book and the old woman beamed with
happiness. "Ah, Heidi!" she said. "What comfort you've brought me!"

Soon after, there was a knock at the window and Heidi saw Grandfather
beckoning her to come home. "I have to go now," she said, "but I'll come again
tomorrow."

She told Grandfather about her plan to buy rolls.

"But wouldn't it be nice for you to have a proper bed?" he said. "There would
still be money to buy the bread. However, the money is yours, Heidi, so you
can do what you like with it. You'll be able to buy bread for Peter's
grandmother for years to come."

Heidi was very happy. "I'm so glad God didn't let me have my way at once,"
she said. "If I'd come home when I first wanted to, I should not have been able
to read, and it's such a comfort to Grandmother. God arranges things so much
better than us, doesn't he, Grandfather?"

"Where did you learn about God, Heidi?" said Grandfather.

"From Clara's grandmother," said Heidi. "She said that God never forgets
us, even if we forget Him."

"Is that right?" said Grandfather, a serious look on his face. "Can we really
go back to God?"

"Oh yes," said Heidi. "There's a beautiful story in my book about a son who

goes away from his father and wastes all his money and everything he had. When he has nothing left, he hires himself out to a man who keeps pigs. The son has to watch the pigs. He has only a few rags to wear and the pigs' food to eat. He thinks about his kind father and longs to go home. And when he does go home, his father doesn't turn him away or blame him for his foolishness. Instead he welcomes him with open arms, and they have feast. Isn't that a beautiful story, Grandfather? I'll read it to you later."

"Yes, Heidi," Grandfather replied softly. "It's a beautiful story."

And after Heidi was asleep that night, Grandfather bowed his head and said a small prayer, and two large tears rolled down his cheeks.

The next day was Sunday. Heidi heard the sound of church bells drifting up from the valley.

"Put on your best frock, Heidi," said Grandfather. "We're going to church together." He was wearing his best coat and trousers.

"Oh, Grandfather!" said Heidi. "You do look nice!"

The church service had begun when Heidi and Grandfather went in through the door of the building. The people were singing a hymn, but soon everyone was nudging each other and whispering, "Did you see? Alm-Uncle is in church!"

And when the service was over, everyone said how friendly he looked and how kindly he behaved towards the child.

Grandfather went to speak to the pastor. "You were right and I was wrong," he said. "I'll find a house in Dorfli for the winter months and Heidi shall go to school."

# The doctor comes to stay

CLARA HAD not been well that Summer. In September the doctor told Herr Sesemann it would be most unwise to take her to Switzerland that year. The doctor himself was a very unhappy man, for both his wife and his only daughter had died from illnesses in the last year. He had grown old and tired-looking during the months since then. Herr Sesemann felt as sorry for him as he did for his own daughter, whom he was going to have to disappoint about the journey to the mountain.

"Doctor, I have an idea," said Herr Sesemann. "Why not make the journey and visit Heidi yourself? The mountain air would do you good, don't you think?"

And that was how the doctor came to be Heidi's first visitor from Frankfurt, and not Clara – who would have to wait until the following Spring when she was stronger. He found a place to stay at Dorfli, but climbed up the mountain to the little hut at the first opportunity.

Heidi welcomed her old friend with a hug. Grandfather also greeted his guest warmly and offered to guide the doctor to any part of the mountains that he would like to see.

Later, after they had eaten golden-brown, toasted cheese and drunk steaming milk from a jug, the doctor said, "Clara must certainly come up here. It would do her a great deal of good."

"Would you like to come out with the goats tomorrow morning?" Heidi asked him.

"Yes, please!" replied the doctor.

So the next morning the doctor came up from Dorfli with Peter and the goats. He tried to talk to the boy, but Peter hardly spoke until they reached the hut where Heidi was waiting for them.

"Are you coming today?" Peter asked her.

"Of course I am," said Heidi.

Grandfather gave Peter the dinner bag, which was heavier than usual, for he had added some meat for the doctor's lunch. Peter grinned when he realised this.

Heidi talked happily about the goats, the flowers, the rocks and the birds as she and the doctor clambered up the slope. Peter sent several unfriendly glances to the doctor, but the doctor did not notice them. They reached Heidi's favourite spot and the doctor sat beside her on the warm grass. The snowfield sparkled in the Autumn sunlight and the rocky peaks stood high against the dark sky.

The doctor sat silently, looking around him. A peaceful feeling came over him as he breathed the fresh air and felt the soft breeze on his face. Everything was so beautiful!

Peter, meanwhile, was feeling cross. It had been several days since Heidi had come up the mountain with him, and now here she sat the whole time beside the old gentleman. Peter could not get a word out of her.

"It's dinner time," he told them after a while.

But the doctor and Heidi only wanted milk to drink, so Peter had all the meat and cheese to himself. This made him feel much more kindly towards the doctor.

It was a bright, sunny Autumn month and the doctor came up the mountain every day. Sometimes Grandfather went with him to the higher slopes and the two enjoyed each other's company enormously. Then September came to an end and it was time for the doctor to return to Frankfurt. He was very sad because the mountain had begun to feel like home to him. "I've learnt how to be happy once more," he told Heidi and her grandfather.

That Winter, Grandfather kept his promise. As soon as the first snow began to fall, he shut up the little hut and went down to Dorfli with Heidi and the goats. He rented an old house near the church which had been empty for a long time. It was badly in need of repair and Grandfather spent most of his time that Winter making it warm and dry.

Heidi went to school in Dorfli every morning and afternoon. She was eager to learn all that was taught her. And when the snow became hard, she was able to go up to Peter's cottage and see his grandmother.

The old lady was not very well and had to stay in bed. "It's only because the frost has gotten into my bones," she told Heidi. She was wearing a shawl to keep her warm and Heidi noticed that her bedclothes were not very thick.

"Your bed isn't right," said Heidi. "Your feet are higher than your head."

"I know." Peter's grandmother moved her thin pillow to make herself more comfortable.

"If only I'd asked Clara to let me take away my Frankfurt bed," said Heidi. "I had three large pillows there."

"Never mind, I'm luckier than many sick people and I should be grateful. Will you read me something today, Heidi?"

So Heidi read some hymns and saw how happy it made the old lady.

"Peter," she said the next day, "you must learn to read."

"I can't," said Peter.

"I'll soon teach you. Then you can read one or two hymns to Grandmother every day."

Teaching Peter to read was hard work. He didn't want to learn and Heidi had to threaten him with all sorts of things. She even told him he would be sent away to a school in Frankfurt if he didn't try to learn.

"Your mother has often spoken to me about the school," she said. "And I used to see the boys going there, all dressed in black."

Peter shuddered at the thought of being sent to a place where you had to wear black clothes and where they forced you to learn things. He tried harder and eventually learned how to read.

One evening, he came into the cottage and said, "I can do it now."

"Do what, Peter?" said his mother.

"Read," he answered.

"Did you hear that, Grandmother?"

Peter fetched the book of hymns and read to his grandmother, who followed the words closely.

"Who would have thought it possible!" said Peter's mother.

At school the next day, when Peter read from this book without the slightest hesitation, the teacher stared at him in astonishment. "How has this miracle come about?" he said.

"It was Heidi," said Peter.

Every evening Peter read to his grandmother, and although she was grateful, she secretly longed for Spring to arrive when Heidi could come and read to her again. For whenever Peter came to a difficult word, he left it out!

# 14

# Clara again!

IT WAS the month of May and clear, warm sunshine lay upon the mountain. The last of the snows had gone and already many of the flowers were springing up through the grass. Heidi was so pleased to be back that she ran round and round Grandfather's hut singing, "On the mountain! On the mountain!"

Then a letter came to tell her that Frau Sesemann was bringing Clara to see her soon! Heidi was delighted, but the prospect of yet another visitor from Frankfurt did not please Peter.

One morning at the end of June, Heidi saw a strange procession making its way up the mountain. In front were two men carrying a sedan chair with a young girl sitting in it. Then there was a horse carrying a stately-looking lady, who was talking to the guide behind her. After this came a wheelchair, pushed by another man, and then a porter carrying a bundle of cloaks, shawls and furs.

"Here they come!" shouted Heidi, jumping with joy.

As the figures came nearer, Heidi rushed forward and the two children hugged each other whilst Frau Sesemann was welcomed by Grandfather. Then the men and the horse went back down the mountain.

"Isn't it lovely, Clara?" said Frau Sesemann.

Clara had never seen anywhere so beautiful. "I'd like to stay here forever!" she said. "Oh, Heidi, if I could only walk with you!"

"I'll push you in your chair," said Heidi. "I'm sure I can."

So Clara was put into her wheelchair and Heidi pushed her round the back of the hut to look at the fir trees. Then she showed her the goat shed, although the goats were with Peter up on the higher slopes.

"I wish I could see Peter and all the goats," sighed Clara, "but we'll have to leave before then."

"Just enjoy all the beautiful things we *can* see," said her grandmother, as she followed the wheelchair which Heidi was pushing further on up the slope.

"Oh, look at those bushes of red flowers!" said Clara.

"If you could come up higher to where the goats are feeding, you would see ever so many more," said Heidi. "And everything looks and smells so lovely up there."

"Grandmother, do you think I could get up there?" said Clara.

"I'm sure I could push the chair up," said Heidi.

Meanwhile, Grandfather had put the table and some extra chairs outside, so that they could eat their dinner in the fresh air. The milk and cheese were soon ready and they sat down for their mid-day meal. Clara ate heartily, much to her grandmother's surprise and pleasure.

"It's the mountain air that gives you an appetite," said Grandfather.

The afternoon went on and Frau Sesemann and Grandfather talked together like old friends. Then she looked towards the west and said, "We must soon get ready to go, Clara. The sun is a good way down and the men will be back with the horse and sedan."

"Oh, just another hour, Grandmother!" begged Clara. "We haven't seen inside the hut yet."

The wheelchair was too wide for the door of the hut, so Grandfather carried Clara inside. She thought Heidi's bedroom in the hay-loft was delightful.

"If you'd agree to it," Grandfather said to Frau Sesemann, "your grand-daughter could stay with us. I'm sure she would grow stronger."

Clara and Heidi were so overjoyed by this suggestion that Frau Sesemann agreed with a smile, and it was decided that Clara should stay for a month.

Later, after Frau Sesemann had gone, Peter came back down the mountain with the goats. The animals quickly flocked round Heidi, who introduced Clara to them. Peter stood sulkily to one side and did not answer when the two girls called out, "Good evening, Peter." Instead, he swung his stick in the air and marched off down the mountain again.

That night, as the girls sat in their hay-loft beds, Clara looked out of the round open window at the clusters of stars in the sky. She hardly ever saw a star in Frankfurt because the curtains were always closed before they came out. Now, Clara stared up at them until her eyes closed and she fell asleep.

Clara had never tasted goat's milk before. When she saw Heidi drinking hers up at breakfast the next morning, she did the same – and found it delicious!

"Tomorrow you can drink two bowls," said Grandfather, smiling.

Peter came with the goats and Grandfather took him to one side.

"Let Little Swan go where she likes," he said. "She knows where to find the best food. A little more climbing won't hurt her and I want her to give the finest milk possible."

Peter nodded and started off with the goats. "Are you coming?" he called to Heidi.

"I can't," she said. "I have to stay here while Clara is with me. But Grandfather has promised to take us both up the mountain one day."

Peter just scowled at Clara and walked on.

The girls ate their meals outside again. As they sat under the fir trees, they exchanged news of all that had happened to them since Heidi had left Frankfurt. The day passed quickly and all at once it was evening. Peter came back with the goats.

"Goodnight, Peter," they called to him, but he did not answer.

Each day, Clara sat in the sun, ate all her food and drank her milk; each night she stared at the stars and slept more soundly than ever before. She was growing stronger and healthier all the time.

One day, Grandfather said to her, "Won't you try and stand for a minute or two?" And Clara made the effort to please him, although her feet hurt when they touched the ground. But each day following this, she tried to stand a little longer.

There was the same cloudless sky each morning and the sun shone brilliantly every day of that Summer. And when evening came the crimson light fell on the mountain peaks and on the great snowfield, until the sun sank in a sea of golden flame.

"Grandfather, will you take us out with the goats tomorrow?" Heidi asked one evening. "It's so lovely up there now."

"Very well," he answered. "But Clara must do her best to stand on her feet again this evening."

Heidi told Peter when he came back with the goats later. "We're all coming with you tomorrow," she said. But Peter just grumbled some reply and swung his stick angrily in the air.

# 15

# Peter and the wheelchair

Grandfather went out early the next morning to see what sort of day it was going to be. There was a light breeze, but the sun was on its way. He wheeled the chair out of the shed, ready for the journey, then went in to call the children.

Peter arrived at that moment. He was in a bad mood, and even the goats seemed to sense this and were keeping away from him. For weeks now he had not had Heidi all to himself as he used to, for each morning she was with the invalid child.

He glared at the wheelchair as if it was an enemy, then looked around. There was no sound anywhere and no one to see him. He sprang forward like a wild animal, caught hold of the chair and gave it a violent push. The chair ran forwards and disappeared over the edge of the slope. Down it went, faster and faster, turning head over heels several times, until finally it was smashed to pieces on the rocks.

Peter laughed and jumped for joy! Now Heidi's friend would *have* to go away because she had no means of getting about. And when she was gone, he would have Heidi to himself.

Soon after, Heidi came running out of the hut and went round to the shed. Grandfather was behind with Clara in his arms. Heidi looked in the shed for the chair.

"Where's the wheelchair, Heidi?" asked Grandfather.

"I can't find it," said Heidi. "I thought you said it was standing outside." Just then, the wind blew the shed door shut. "The wind must have blown it away! Oh, if it's blown it all the way down to Dorfli, we'll never get it back in time to go up the mountain!"

"If it's rolled that far, it will be in a hundred pieces by now," said Grandfather. "But it's a strange thing to have happened."

Clara was very upset. "I'll have to go home if I have no chair."

Grandfather tried to calm her. "I'll carry you up the mountain," he said. "Later on, we'll see what can be done."

When they reached the spot where the goats usually pastured, Peter was already there.

"Have you seen anything of the wheelchair?" Grandfather asked him.

"What wheelchair?" said Peter.

Grandfather said no more. He spread some shawls on the grass and put Clara down on them.

"Oh, this is lovely! Lovely!" she cried, looking round.

Grandfather said he would come and fetch them that evening, and he went off down the mountain again.

The sky was dark blue and there was not a cloud to be seen. The great snowfield overhead sparkled as if set with thousands and thousands of gold and silver stars. The goats had become used to Clara and several of them came across to rub their heads against her shoulder.

Heidi left her with them for a short while and wandered higher, where the flowers were thick under her feet and where they smelled sweetest. She breathed in the delicious scent then ran back to Clara. "You must come!" she said. "It's more beautiful than you can imagine. I'm sure I could carry you."

"But Heidi, you're smaller than I am!" said Clara. "Oh, if only I could walk!"

Then Heidi had an idea. "Peter!" she called. "Come here!"

"No!" shouted Peter.

"If you don't, I'll do something you don't like," Heidi told him.

Peter was suddenly afraid that Heidi might know something about the wheelchair and was threatening to tell her grandfather. He went down to the two girls.

Heidi told him to take hold of Clara under her arm and then she did the same the other side. Together they lifted her. Then Clara put one arm around Heidi's shoulder and the other through Peter's arm.

"Put your foot down firmly," Heidi told Clara. "I'm sure it won't hurt so much after that."

And she was right. Slowly, Clara put one foot in front of the other and moved across the grass. "I can do it!" she cried. "Look, Heidi, I can make proper steps!"

"Yes!" shouted Heidi. "You're walking, Clara! You're walking!"

After a while, they reached the field of flowers and sat down. The flowers waved to and fro in the soft breeze and their sweet scent filled the air. Clara was almost overcome with happiness.

Peter lay back on the ground and fell asleep, but his dreams were full of wheelchairs! He woke up sweating. And when it was time to take Clara back to where Grandfather would meet them, he didn't complain once.

All three were hungry, but only Heidi and Clara ate their dinners and drank their milk with enjoyment. Peter's appetite was spoiled by the worry of what was going to happen about the wheelchair.

When Grandfather came to fetch them, Heidi rushed to tell him the good news about Clara.

"So we made the effort and won the day!" he said to Clara, smiling.

Then he lifted her up and put a strong arm around her and she walked even more confidently than before.

When Peter got to Dorfli that evening, people were talking about the wheelchair. They were standing in a group around the broken object.

"It must be worth a lot of money," said one man. "I can't think how such an accident could have happened."

"Alm-Uncle said the wind might have done it," said a woman.

"No doubt the gentleman from Frankfurt will want to know what happened," said the man. "He's bound to be suspicious of anyone who was up the mountain at that time."

Peter crept away and then ran home as fast as he could. He was certain that any day a policeman would come from Frankfurt and he would be put in prison.

# 16

# Surprises!

THE FOLLOWING days were some of the happiest that Clara had spent on the mountain. She awoke each morning thinking, "I am well now! I can walk by myself like other people!" Because after several days of trying, she *could* walk on her own and every day she was able to walk a little further.

Then came the time for her grandmother's second visit. The day before, Peter brought a letter from Frau Sesemann, saying that she would arrive as expected. Peter handed the letter to Grandfather and then turned away quickly and ran off up the mountain with the goats.

"Why does Peter act as if somebody was after him with a big stick?" said Heidi.

"Perhaps because he thinks the stick which he so well deserves is coming after him," said Grandfather thoughtfully.

They began to prepare for Frau Sesemann's arrival. Heidi tidied the hut, then the two girls dressed themselves and went to sit on the seat outside to wait for her. Grandfather joined them, holding some blue flowers which he had gathered from the mountain-side.

At last, Frau Sesemann's procession came up the slope. First came the guide, then the white horse with the lady herself and last of all the porter, with a bundle of wraps and rugs on his back.

Frau Sesemann had no sooner got off the horse when she said, "Clara! Why aren't you in your chair?" She looked more closely. "Is it really you? Your cheeks have grown quite round and rosy. I should hardly have known you."

She was walking towards them when both Heidi and Clara stood up. Then Clara put a hand on Heidi's shoulder and the two girls began walking along quite easily and naturally. Frau Sesemann could hardly believe it! Laughing and crying at the same time, she hurried forward and hugged both of them in turn. Then she turned towards Grandfather, who was smiling.

"How much we have to thank you for!" she said to him, warmly. "It's all your care and nursing – "

"And God's good sun and mountain air," he said.

"And the delicious milk I've been drinking," said Clara.

"My son must come here at once," said Frau Sesemann. "I must send a telegram to Paris without delay. I won't say why. It will be a wonderful surprise for him. Now, how can I send a telegram? The guide and the porter have gone already."

"I'll fetch Peter," said Grandfather. "He can take it for you."

He went to one side and blew a loud whistle which echoed in the rocks overhead. After a few minutes, Peter came running down. He looked as white as a ghost, expecting to see a policeman waiting for him. But Grandfather

gave him a piece of paper and told him to take it to the post office in Dorfli.

Meanwhile, Herr Sesemann, who had finished his business in Paris, had also been preparing a surprise. Without saying a word to his mother, he got on the train one sunny morning and went to Basle. Next day, he went on to Mayenfield, and then by carriage to Dorfli. And at the very moment Peter was coming down the mountain with the telegram message, Herr Sesemann was climbing *up* the mountain to see his daughter.

"Is this the way to the hut where the old man and Heidi live, and where the visitors from Frankfurt are staying?" he asked the boy.

But Peter just ran on with a frightened cry and fell head over heels, rolling and bumping down the slope. The telegram message was torn to pieces and blew away.

'How strange these mountain people are,' thought Herr Sesemann as he climbed on towards the hut.

Peter rolled on down, so afraid that he barely noticed the bumps and bruises to his body. He was sure that the stranger who had asked the way was the policeman from Frankfurt. At last he came to a halt, caught up in a bush, and he lay still for several seconds, catching his breath. He would have liked to go home and creep into bed, but he had left the goats on the mountain and Alm-Uncle had told him to hurry back to them. So he pulled himself to his feet and began the climb.

Herr Sesemann was almost there. He could see the hut ahead of him and in another minute or two he would be surprising his little daughter with his arrival. But the people above had seen him coming and they were preparing their own surprise for him.

As he came closer to the hut, two figures came towards him. One of them was a tall girl with fair hair and pink cheeks. She was leaning on Heidi, whose eyes were dancing with joy. Herr Sesemann stopped and stared at the two children. Suddenly there were tears in his eyes. The fair-haired girl looked so like Clara's mother that he did not know whether he was awake or dreaming.

"Don't you know me, Papa?" Clara called to him.

Then Herr Sesemann ran to his child and took her in his arms. "How is it possible? Is it true what I see? Are you really my little Clara?"

Frau Sesemann came forward. "What do you say now, dear son?" she said. "You have given us a pleasant surprise, but we have given you an even bigger one. But you must come and pay your respects to Heidi's grandfather, who has been such a help to Clara."

"Yes, indeed," said Herr Sesemann. "And here is dear little Heidi! It's a pleasure to see you."

A minute later, he and Grandfather were shaking hands and Herr Sesemann was expressing his heartfelt thanks to the old man.

There was a slight rustling in the bushes as Peter arrived. He had tried to slip by without being seen, but Frau Sesemann called him across. Heidi had not told her who had picked the blue flowers for her and she wondered if Peter had. She wanted to thank him, but he seemed reluctant to come over.

"Come along, boy," she said. "Don't be afraid. Tell me, was it you who did it?"

Peter was looking at the ground and did not see Frau Sesemann pointing at the bunch of blue flowers. He knew that Grandfather was now watching him closely, with the stranger from Frankfurt – the policeman – by his side.

Shaking all over, Peter said, "Yes," very quietly.

"Well, what is so dreadful about that?" said Frau Sesemann.

"B-because it's broken to pieces and nobody can put it back together again," said Peter.

"Is the boy a little out of his mind?" she asked Grandfather.

"No," said Grandfather, who had suspected the true reason for the accident with the wheelchair from the beginning. "*He* was the 'wind' that sent the wheelchair down the slope and he's waiting for his punishment."

"Oh!" said Frau Sesemann. "Well, we won't punish the poor boy any more. Let's be fair. He was angry when we all came here and began to take Heidi away from him – or that was how he saw it. We all do foolish things when we're angry." She went across to Peter. "Now stop shaking and listen," she said to him. "What you did was very wrong, as you now know. But things have turned out for the best. When Clara had no chair to ride in, she made the effort to walk and every day since then she's been walking better and better. Now it's over and done with and I'd like you to have something as a *pleasant* reminder of the visitors from Frankfurt. What would you like as a present?"

Peter was astonished. He had expected something dreadful to happen to him and now he was being offered a present! What should he have? Then he remembered the yearly fair at Mayenfield where there were lots of stalls, packed with pretty things to buy. There were little red whistles that he could use to call his goats and splendid knives with round handles. If he had a penny, he could choose.

"A penny," he said.

Frau Sesemann could not help laughing. "Come here then." And she put a pile of pennies into his hand. "I've given you as many pennies as there are weeks in the year," she explained. Every Sunday you can take a penny out to spend."

Peter looked at the money and said, "Thank you!" Then he ran off up the mountain, jumping for joy.

Herr Sesemann turned to Grandfather. "I'm a rich man, but money couldn't buy the thing I wanted most – my daughter's health. But you've made her strong. I can never really repay you for that, but I want to give you something. Tell me, what can I give you?"

"I have enough for the child and myself for as long as I live," said Grandfather. "But I'm growing old and shan't be here much longer. The child has no relations, except for one person who will always try to make a profit out of her. If you could promise me that Heidi will never want for anything, or have to earn her living among strangers, that will richly reward me for what I've done for Clara."

"I look upon Heidi as if she were my own daughter," Herr Sesemann told him. "And I promise to protect her always." He turned to Heidi. "Now tell me, is there anything you wish for?"

"Yes, there is," said Heidi. "I'd like the bed I slept in at Frankfurt, with the high pillows and the thick cover, then Peter's grandmother won't have to lie with her head lower than her feet and hardly be able to breathe. She'll be warm and comfortable in it."

"I'll send a telegram to Fraulein Rottenmeier," said Herr Sesemann, looking surprised. "The bed will be here the day after tomorrow!"

Heidi skipped around with glee. "How wonderful! I must go and tell Grandmother. She'll be so pleased!"

Frau Sesemann laughed. "Let's *all* go and tell her!" she said.

And minutes later, a very happy party of people set off down the mountain. But Heidi was the happiest of them all.